JUDITH CASELEY

Harry
and
Willy
and
Carrothead

Greenwillow Books, New York

A black pen line was combined with watercolor paints
and colored pencils for the full-color art.
The text type is ITC Esprit Book.
Copyright © 1991 by Judith Caseley
Manufactured in China.
11 12 13 SCP 20 19 18 17 16 15 14 13 12
First Edition

Library of Congress Cataloging-in-Publication Data
Caseley, Judith.
Harry and Willy and Carrothead / Judith Caseley.
p.   cm.
Summary: Three boys overcome prejudicial ideas
about appearances and become friends.
ISBN 0-688-09492-9. ISBN 0-688-09493-7 (lib. bdg.)
[1. Physically handicapped—Fiction.
2. Friendship—Fiction.]   I. Title.
PZ7.C2677Har   1991
[E]—dc20   90-30291   CIP   AC

To Daniel Munz
and friends
at P.S. 205,
with special thanks
to Jack Lenze, C.P.O.

WITHDRAWN

When Harry was born he had no left hand. His left arm stopped at the elbow. In his first photograph he was all bundled up, and you couldn't even tell.

At first his parents were sad and scared.
But when they took him home, he cried and cooed
and waved his arms like any baby.

When Harry's mother wheeled him in the
carriage, a neighbor looked at Harry and
said, "The poor little thing."
"He's a wonderful baby," said Harry's mother.

When Harry was one, he learned to run.
His mother said he never bothered walking.

Harry climbed out of his crib and slept on the floor.
His father said he had a mind of his own, right
from the start.

When Harry was older, he learned to fingerpaint.
He made great designs with his hand and his arm.
"How beautiful," said his mother, and she put one
of his pictures in a frame on the living room wall.

When Harry was four, he was fitted
for a prosthesis.
When he was five, he started school.
The children gathered around him.
"What's wrong with your arm?" said a boy with
red hair, pointing to Harry's left arm.
"Nothing," said Harry. "That's my prosthesis."
"Can I touch it?" said a boy named Willy.
"Sure," said Harry, and he held out his arm.

At snacktime the children watched Harry eat.

He ate a banana.

He ate some raisins.

He ate three chocolate chip cookies.

"Just like a regular kid," said the boy with red hair.

"Sure," said Harry. "What's your name?"

"My name is Oscar," said the boy.

"But we call him Carrothead," said Willy.

Oscar made a funny face, but he didn't say anything.

Harry and Oscar sat next to each other in the
classroom.
They made monster masks out of brown paper bags.
They whispered to each other, and the teacher
shushed them.

Once Harry made an airplane and threw it to Oscar,
and Harry got caught. The teacher made him stay
inside when the children went to the playground.
Oscar stayed, too, to keep him company.

One day they played ball in the schoolyard.
Harry held out his arms.
"Throw!" he said.
Oscar threw the ball gently, as if he thought
Harry was a baby.
"My arm won't break," said Harry, laughing,
and Oscar threw a fastball.
Harry was a great ballplayer. Almost as
good as Willy.

At Halloween there was a party at school. Harry was the Tin Man from *The Wizard of Oz*, with a silver funnel on his head. He even painted his five fingernails silver. He didn't paint his prosthesis, because his mother wouldn't like it.

Oscar was the Scarecrow.

"Hey, Carrothead," said Willy, who was dressed like a pirate. "You should have been a pumpkin with that orange hair."

Oscar didn't answer.

But Harry did.

"Call him Oscar," said Harry.

Willy took out his pirate's sword and said,

"Who's going to make me?"

Harry doubled his fist and lifted his

left arm. He was ready to fight.

"I am," he said.

Willy stood there for a moment, and then he said,
"Want to hold my parrot, Oscar?"

Now Harry and Oscar and Willy are friends.

Willy and Harry play a lot of ball together.

Harry's hero is Jim Abbott.

And me? Well, my name is Oscar, and I'm the best writer in the class. That's why I wrote this story about Harry and Willy and Carrothead—

except nobody calls me that anymore.